Agent Secret stood in Spy Headquarters sipping his juice box. He was a spy who liked his adventure exciting and his juice boxes . . . shaken.

"Agent Secret, the world needs your help," said his boss, Miss T. "Your assignment is to retrieve three secret containers."

"Will there be danger?" asked Agent Secret. "And dancing?"

"Of course," said Miss T.

Meanwhile the evil Lady in Pink and her henchman Tyrone had their own plans.

"We need to get those containers first," said the Lady in Pink.

"What's inside?" asked Henchman Tyrone.

"You might call it . . . a recipe for disaster," answered the Lady in Pink. "Heh, heh, heh," she laughed evilly. "You're supposed to laugh, too, Henchman."

"Oh, right," said Henchman Tyrone. "Heh, heh, heh."

At an ice-cream pub in London, Secret Contact Austin gave Agent Secret a computer hidden in a banana split. The computer told Agent Secret where to find the first container.

Agent Secret went to the Glass Building in London and danced the correct sequence to get the container. The Lady in Pink tried to snatch it away from him, but she was no match for Agent Secret!

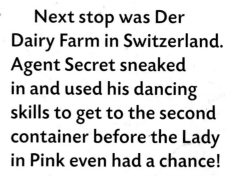

Next stop was Der Dairy Farm in Switzerland. Agent Secret sneaked in and used his dancing skills to get to the second container before the Lady in Pink even had a chance!

"This is too easy," said Agent Secret as he zoomed away in a snowmobile.

But on Tiki Island the Lady in Pink and Henchman Tyrone had a plan. They arrived at the secret location of the third container *before* Agent Secret!

 While Henchman Tyrone guarded the entrance, the Lady in Pink tiptoed through a cave and punched a button on a giant Tiki face. A computer sprang to life.

 "Begin dance sequence to unlock vault," the computer bleeped. The music started. The Lady in Pink started dancing.

The Lady in Pink danced every step right.
"Dance sequence incomplete," the computer said.

Before she could argue, Agent Secret stepped out of the shadows. Agent Secret, the Lady in Pink, and Henchman Tyrone danced. Their feet moved faster and faster, hitting every step right.

They struck a pose at the end of the song. "Dance complete," said the computer.

The vault opened. The third container appeared!

"You are a very good dancer," said Agent Secret.
"I am not good!" said the Lady in Pink. "I am *evil*!"
She snatched the container and ran for the exit.
"Clever," said Agent Secret.

Outside, the Lady in Pink and Henchman Tyrone tried to make their getaway.

Agent Secret revved his speedboat and caught up with them in no time.

"Faster, Henchman! Faster!" shouted the Lady in Pink.

It was too late. Agent Secret had already grabbed the container.
"I'd love to stay," said Agent Secret, "but I really must jet."
"Jet?" said the Lady in Pink and Henchman Tyrone.
With the press of a button Agent Secret's speedboat sprouted wings and he flew off!

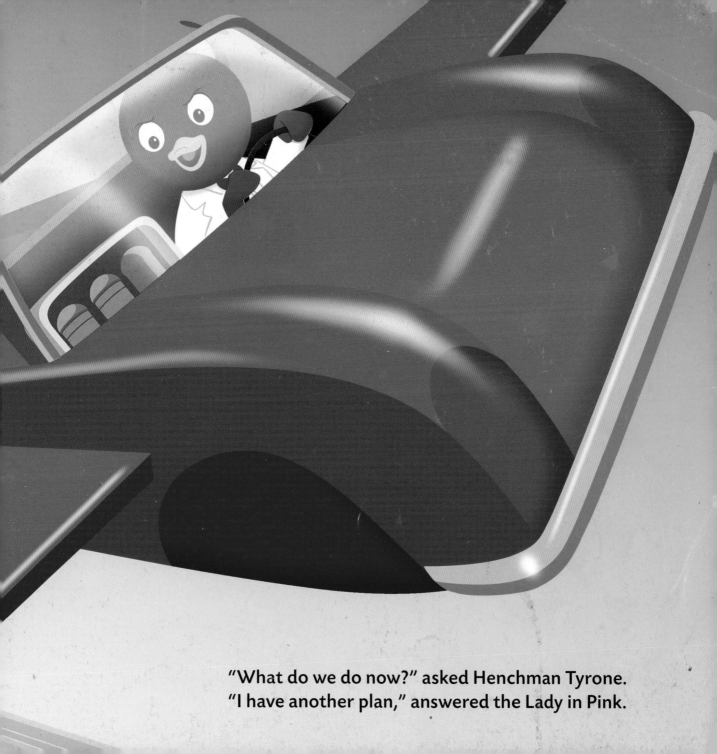

"What do we do now?" asked Henchman Tyrone.
"I have another plan," answered the Lady in Pink.

Agent Secret returned to headquarters. "Miss T, I have the containers!" he announced.

But Miss T was not there! Just then the Lady in Pink popped up on the screen.

"Bring the containers to my secret hideout in the clock tower," she said, "or Miss T gets the tickle table! Heh, heh, heh."

Agent Secret had no choice. But he did have a plan.

He pressed a button, and Secret Contact Austin appeared on the screen. "I need your help, Secret Contact Austin," he said. "And bring a pizza."

"Free Miss T," Agent Secret commanded as soon as he arrived at the hideout.

"Hand over the containers first," the Lady in Pink replied.

But as soon as Agent Secret did, a second tickle table scooped him up. It was a trap!

"Now before I tickle you both," said the Lady in Pink, "let's see what's inside these containers."

Inside the first container was a drinking glass . . . inside the second was milk . . .

Before she could open the third container, the doorbell rang.

"Did someone order a pizza?" Secret Contact Austin asked.
"Mmmm, pizza," said Henchman Tyrone.
"Wait!" said the Lady in Pink. "He's with them. He's a good guy!"
She grabbed the third container and made a run for it. Henchman
Tyrone followed.

Secret Contact Austin helped free Miss T and Agent Secret. They chased the evildoers onto the roof.

"Stand back," shouted the Lady in Pink as she opened the third container.

Inside was chocolate syrup!

"Aha!" she shouted. "Now I can make chocolate milk, all for *me*!"

Just then the clock rang out. *Dong! Dong!*

The Lady in Pink dropped the chocolate syrup!

"Noooo!" the Lady in Pink wailed. Suddenly she lost her balance and fell!

Agent Secret thought fast. "Give me that pizza box," he said to Secret Contact Austin.

The pizza box was really a jet pack!

"Cool, huh?" said Agent Secret. He swooped down and caught the Lady in Pink and the chocolate syrup!

"Maybe we could share the chocolate milk," said the Lady in Pink.

"Sure," answered Agent Secret. "Now that it's . . . shaken."

Back at the secret hideout they all shared the chocolate milk.
"We make a good team," said Agent Secret. "It's too bad you're evil."
"Well, maybe it's time to try being good," said the Lady in Pink.
"I certainly didn't expect that!" said Secret Contact Austin.
"I did," answered Agent Secret. "I always expect the unexpected."